Almost ANYTHING

Sophy Henn

It was the sort of day for doing almost anything
and everyone was busy with this and that.

Everyone except George.
George didn't think he could
do this *or* that . . .

So George did nothing.

"Hello, George," said Otter.
"And what are you up to?"

"Oh . . . nothing," said George.

"Well, why don't you come and do some
painting with me?" said Otter.

"That does look good," said George. "But I can't paint."

"Come and do some dancing
with us then!" said Hedgehog.

"That does sound fun,"
said George.
"But I can't dance."

Then Badger asked George if he
might like to play skittles.

"That does look smashing,"
said George. "Only,
I can't play skittles."

"You could help me
fly my kite," said Fox.

"Or try a spot of roller skating?" said Beaver.

"I'd love to . . . but I can't," said George rather sadly.
"My paws are too fumbly for flying kites
and I can't do roller skating.
I'm a little bit wobbly."

So George did nothing.

Now Bear, who had watched all of this, was as smart
as she was old – and she was very old.

She took a sheet of paper, folded it
once, twice and three times more.

"George," said Bear. "Come over here.
I have something for you . . ."

"For me?" asked George.

"For you," said Bear as she
handed him a small paper hat.
"It's magic."

"Really?" asked George.

"Really," said Bear. "If you wear this hat,
I am quite sure you will be able to do
almost anything, *even* roller skating."

"But, Bear, I can't . . ."

"You can, George," said Bear.
"Just pop the hat on . . ."

So George did pop the hat on,
and the roller skates.
And off he went . . .

"Oh, Bear!" cried George.
"You said if I wore the magic hat
I could do almost anything . . .

but I can't!
I'm just too wobbly!"

"Of course you can," said Bear. "You just
need to give the magic a chance.
Have another go, George."

So George gave the magic
a chance and he
had another go.

And after a time he found he *was* roller skating!

"Hooray! The magic hat is working!"
said George. "I wonder what else it can do . . ."

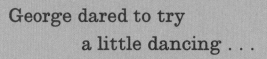

George dared to try
a little dancing . . .

And in no time at all he found that
his footwork was quite fancy indeed.

"Well, how about that?" said George. "I can dance!"

George leapt and twirled and jigged
until his feet felt weary. And then
he tried a spot of painting . . .

"Hurrah!" said George.
"I can paint!"

After all that, George thought
he might try a little bit of reading.

"Look, Bear, look at me . . . I'm reading!"
said George. "Oh, thank you, Bear.
I love my magic hat!"

And just like that
George found he was
extremely busy . . .

doing this . . .

and that . . .

and more besides . . .

until . . .

OOOOOOOO!"

cried George.
"Oh, Bear, the hat is lost!
The magic is gone.
And now I can't do
almost anything."

"Don't worry," said Bear. "The hat may be lost,
but the magic *isn't* gone. You see, George,
that hat was only folded-up paper.
The magic — that came from you!"

"I'm magic?" asked George.

"You are," said Bear. "Just think of all
those wonderful things you did . . .

. . . with *and* without the hat.

George, when you give your
magic a chance, you can do
almost anything."

"I can?" said George.
"I can!"

And once George knew this,
    he tried ever so hard to always
        give his magic a chance . . .

Even when he was a little bit wobbly!

PUFFIN BOOKS

UK | USA | Canada | Ireland | Australia | India | New Zealand | South Africa
Puffin Books is part of the Penguin Random House group of companies
whose addresses can be found at global.penguinrandomhouse.com.
www.penguin.co.uk   www.puffin.co.uk   www.ladybird.co.uk

Penguin
Random House
UK

First published 2018
001

Printed in China
A CIP catalogue record for this book is available from the British Library
Hardback ISBN: 978–0–141–37074–3
Paperback ISBN: 978–0–141–38547–1
All correspondence to: Puffin Books, Penguin Random House Children's
80 Strand, London WC2R 0RL

MIX
Paper from
responsible sources
FSC
www.fsc.org
FSC® C018179